JEWEL KINGDOM

Scholastic Inc. 557 Broadway New York, NY 10012 • PO # 5012797 (05/20)

JEWEL KINGDOM

The Diamond Princess
Saves the Day

THE WHITE WINTERLAND

THE VALLEY OF
THE DRAGONS

SECRET
CAVE

THE GREAT WALL

APPLESAP AND
MARIGOLD'S
COTTAGE

BUTTERCUP
MEADOW

JEWEL PALACE

THE RUBY
PALACE

BLUE
BONNET
FALLS

DEEP
DARK

THE RED
MOUNTAINS

RUSHING RIVER

BLUE LAKE

THE SAPPHIRE
PALACE

READ ALL THE
JEWEL KINGDOM
BOOKS!

#1: The Ruby Princess
Runs Away

#2: The Sapphire Princess
Meets a Monster

#3: The Emerald Princess
Plays a Trick

#4: The Diamond Princess
Saves the Day

JEWEL KINGDOM

The Diamond Princess
Saves the Day

by Jahnna N. Malcolm

Illustrations by Sumiti Collina

Scholastic Inc.

Copyright © 2020 by Jahnna Beecham and Malcolm Hillgartner
Illustrations by Sumiti Collina copyright © 2020 by Scholastic Inc.
All rights reserved. Published by Scholastic Inc., *Publishers since 1920*. SCHOLASTIC and associated logos are trademarks and/or registered trademarks of Scholastic Inc.

This book is a work of fiction. Names, characters, places, and incidents are either the product of the author's imagination or are used fictitiously, and any resemblance to actual persons, living or dead, business establishments, events, or locales is entirely coincidental.

ISBN 978-1-338-56573-7

10 9 8 7 6 5 4 3 2 1   20 21 22 23 24

Printed in the U.S.A.   40
First printing 2020
Book design by Maeve Norton

For Chris Tomasino and
her Diamond Princess, Nora

1

ON THE ICE

"Put on your skates and follow me," Demetra called to her cousin. "Hurry!"

The Diamond Princess was dressed in her favorite white velvet skating skirt and jacket. She slipped on her silver skates and leaped lightly onto the crystal pond. Then she skated as fast as she could toward the center of the ice, her hair flying behind her.

"Demetra, don't skate so fast," Sabrina shouted after her. "You're much better at this than I am. We don't do any skating where I live."

Sabrina was the Sapphire Princess. She lived in her palace at Blue Lake. It was a watery world of weeping willows and lily pads.

This was the total opposite of Demetra's kingdom. Her palace sat in the heart of the White Winterland, a world of ice and snow.

"I have something very important to ask you." Demetra spun around to face Sabrina. "But I don't want any of my people to hear."

"Is it about Winterfest?" Sabrina asked.

Winterfest, which would begin that evening, was one of the biggest events in the White Winterland. The festival was three wonderful days filled with music, dance, and feasts.

"Winterfest is fine," Demetra said. "It's Finley who's the problem."

Finley was a fluffy white fox who held the important job of being Demetra's palace advisor.

"What's happened?" Sabrina asked, catching hold of her cousin's arm. "Did you two have a fight?"

Demetra sighed. "All we do is fight."

"Oh, Demetra, that's terrible," Sabrina said. "How long has this been going on?"

"Practically since the day I was crowned the Diamond Princess," Demetra replied. "But it's gotten much worse since we started planning Winterfest."

"What do you fight about?" Sabrina asked.

"Everything," Demetra said, raising her hands in frustration. "This morning we fought over who would judge the ice sculptures.

And this afternoon we argued over where we would serve the hot cider and cookies after the ice show."

Sabrina tapped her chin with one mittened hand. "I don't like the sound of this."

"Me, neither." Demetra folded her arms across her chest. "I thought Finley was supposed to be my friend."

"He is," Sabrina replied. "Just like Zazz the butterfly is my friend and advisor."

Demetra nodded. "And Hapgood the dragon is Roxanne's friend and advisor."

"And Arden the unicorn is Emily's," Sabrina added.

Roxanne and Emily were their cousins, the Ruby and Emerald princesses. They had all grown up at the Jewel Palace until King Regal and Queen Gemma gave each girl her own kingdom to rule. Roxanne was given the Red Mountains, and Emily reigned over the Greenwood.

"Then what's the matter with Finley?" Demetra asked.

"Maybe the problem isn't just Finley?" Sabrina said, pursing her lips. "Maybe it's you, too."

Demetra looked curious. "Me?"

Sabrina nodded. "Sometimes you can be a teensy bit bossy."

"Bossy!" Demetra gasped.

"When we were growing up," Sabrina continued, "you used to order Roxanne and Emily around all the time. And they didn't like it one bit."

Demetra dug at the ice with the toe of her skate but said nothing.

"Remember, you have to be a friend to have one," Sabrina reminded her.

"Well, maybe I am a little bossy," Demetra finally confessed. "But so is Finley. He thinks he knows everything about Winterfest."

"Finley probably does know a lot," Sabrina pointed out. "He grew up here. And this is your first Winterfest."

"But that doesn't give him the right to call me names," Demetra protested. "This morning he said I was just a pigheaded princess!"

"What!" Sabrina exclaimed in surprise. "That's not a very nice thing to say."

"Princess Demetra!" a familiar voice shouted from behind them. It startled Demetra so much she nearly fell down.

"Finley!" Demetra gasped when she was finally able to turn around. The white fox was standing on the ice behind her.

As upset as she was with Finley, Demetra didn't want him to know she'd been talking about him. "How long have you been there?"

"I only just got here," Finley replied stiffly. "I have a message to deliver."

Demetra responded in the same stiff way. "What is your message?"

"There seems to be a problem at Sparkle Mountain." Finley pointed to the sky in the west. An odd greenish cloud had formed a circle around the tallest peak.

Demetra had never seen anything like it before. She forgot all about being angry with Finley and concentrated on her job as princess.

"This is very strange," she declared. "I had better go see what's the matter."

Finley nodded. "I've already arranged for a sleigh to take you to Sparkle Mountain."

The tinkling of harness bells rang in the crisp air as Rolf the reindeer pulled the crystal sleigh up beside them.

"Sabrina, will you oversee the rest of the Winterfest preparations?" Demetra asked.

Sabrina nodded. "You can count on me."

Demetra hurried to the crystal sleigh, but Finley hopped in ahead of her.

"I'm coming with you," the fox said.

Demetra put her hands on her hips. "I'm

sorry, Finley, but you have to stay here. Sabrina needs your help."

"You're the one who needs my help," Finley said. "The road to Sparkle Mountain is very tricky."

Demetra sighed. "I'm sure Rolf and I can figure it out. Now please get out of the sleigh."

Finley shook his head stubbornly. "You won't be able to find the path up the mountain. It's hidden. I'm the one who knows how to find it."

"I think you should take Finley," Princess Sabrina cut in. "If the road is confusing and the path so easy to miss, it sounds like you will need him."

Finley sat back in the seat. "Then it's settled."

Demetra stared at her cousin in shock. As she climbed into the sleigh, she whispered, "I can't believe you took Finley's side."

"I'm not taking sides," Sabrina whispered back. "I just think two heads are better than one. And I don't want you to get lost, Demetra. Not when the guests are about to arrive for Winterfest."

Demetra knew her cousin was right. With

a frustrated sigh, she picked up the reins and opened her mouth to give directions to the reindeer.

But Finley spoke first. "Rolf, let's take the back route along Glacier's Edge. It's much faster. Giddy up!"

As the reindeer clip-clopped across the frozen lake, Demetra turned and made a face at her cousin. "See?"

Sabrina cupped her hands around her mouth and called, "Remember, work together!"

2

TROUBLE AT SPARKLE MOUNTAIN

When the princess and the fox reached the foot of Sparkle Mountain, the cloud had grown. It now covered the mountain like a sickly green fog.

"Where's the path?" Demetra asked, squinting through the mist.

Finley scampered forward onto Rolf's back. "I'm not really sure," he called.

"Not sure?" Demetra huffed. "But you said

you were the only one who knew how to find it!"

"I *would* know how to find it in good weather," Finley shot back. "But right now, I can barely see my paw in front of my nose!"

"We had better go look for it," Demetra said, hopping out of the sleigh. Then she

called to the reindeer, "Wait for us here, Rolf."

"As you wish, Princess," Rolf replied.

Demetra and Finley inched into the green mist. They hadn't gone more than ten feet when they froze. Someone was crying. Quite close by.

"I don't know what to do," a little voice moaned. "I'm such a coward."

"Someone's in trouble," Finley whispered.

The princess and the fox tiptoed forward, following the sound. They climbed up the steep, snow-covered slope. Then they passed between two large boulders frosted over with pale green ice.

When Demetra and Finley found the owner of the voice, they nearly tripped over her. She was a tiny white bunny huddled in the middle of the path.

"Why, look, it's Alpenglow," Demetra cried.

The bunny looked up at the princess with frightened eyes. "I wanted to help but couldn't," she whimpered.

"Help who?" the princess asked.

"Elsinor and the other goblins," Alpenglow explained. "They're trapped inside Sparkle Mountain."

"What were they doing in there?" Finley asked.

"Mining for rock crystal," Alpenglow whimpered. "It was to be a surprise for you, Princess. In honor of Winterfest."

"Oh dear," Demetra replied. "This is terrible. Can you tell us what happened?"

"I heard a loud crashing sound. Then the mountain started rumbling." Alpenglow sobbed. "I wanted to help the goblins, but I couldn't. I was too frightened."

Demetra placed one hand on Alpenglow's head. The bunny was shaking so hard her teeth chattered. "There was nothing you could do," Demetra said, offering the bunny her cape. "Don't blame yourself."

"It sounds like they've had a cave-in," Finley whispered to Demetra.

The princess nodded. "Elsinor and his goblins could be buried under the rocks."

"Use your Magic Mirror," Finley said, tugging on Demetra's arm.

"I planned on doing that," she replied.

Actually, the news about the goblins was so upsetting that Demetra had forgotten she was carrying the Magic Mirror.

"Look into it and see if the goblins are hurt," the white fox urged.

"I will!"

Demetra didn't like it when Finley barked orders at her. It made her flustered.

She fumbled for the Magic Mirror. It had been given to her by the great wizard Gallivant on the day she was crowned the Diamond Princess. The mirror gave Demetra the power to see people and things in other places.

Finley tugged on her sleeve again. "Remember, you can only use it three times in one day."

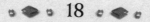

"I know that," Demetra snapped at Finley. He was really starting to irritate her.

She took two steps away from him and raised the shimmering glass into the air. The diamonds on its handle sparkled in the mist.

"Oh, Magic Mirror, so shiny bright,
Show me the goblins. Are they all right?"

The silver mirror suddenly turned into a reflecting pool. Demetra could see Elsinor and two other lavender goblins huddled together on a large white mound. Big rock crystals were scattered around them.

"Can you see them?" Finley asked.

Demetra nodded. "They don't appear to be hurt. But they look scared."

 19

"Where are they?" Finley asked.

"I'm not sure," Demetra said with a frown. "They're surrounded by crystals."

"Can you see anything else?" Finley asked.

Demetra looked back at the mirror, but the image had disappeared. "No."

"Well, what should we do?" Finley asked.

Demetra pursed her lips. "We have to go in," she said finally.

"But how do you plan to get inside?" Finley waved his paw in the mist. "We can't even see the mine entrance."

Alpenglow raised herself up on her hind legs and pointed. "It's right behind you."

"Oh!" Finley spun around quickly, then backed away from the big wooden door.

"What's the matter, Finley?" Demetra asked.

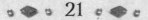

Finley stared at the mine entrance. "Ever since I was a little kit, I was warned never to go into Sparkle Mountain. Something awful hides inside there."

"Like what?" Demetra whispered.

Finley twisted his fluffy tail nervously in his paws. "I'm not sure. But I hear terrible things happen to you if you go inside."

Demetra was surprised. Finley, who was usually so cocky, actually sounded frightened.

"Elsinor and the goblins weren't afraid to go inside the mountain," Demetra pointed out.

"And look what happened to them!" Finley rasped.

Finley's words made little goose bumps creep up Demetra's arms.

"Listen, Finley," she said, taking a deep breath. "If it scares you so much, I'll go into the mountain by myself. You can wait with Alpenglow and Rolf in the sleigh."

"I am *not* scared," Finley sputtered. He puffed up his chest, trying to act brave. "And I will *not* wait in the sleigh. I'm going with you. In fact," he added, marching into the mist, "I'll lead the way."

3

HUNTING FOR GOBLINS

Two tunnels lay behind the big wooden door. The one to the right was very large and very dark. The one to the left was much smaller but glistened with light.

"I think we should take the lit tunnel," Demetra declared.

Finley shook his head firmly. "We have to be cautious, Princess. We don't know what's down there. We could get trapped. I say we take the big tunnel."

Demetra put her hands on her hips. "But the big tunnel is so dark. We don't know what's down there, either."

The fox rapped on the rock with his paw. "Yes, but this rock is solid and would never collapse."

The princess peeked inside the black tunnel and shivered. It was dark. Demetra wouldn't admit it to Finley, but she was afraid of the dark.

"That little tunnel is bright and shiny," she declared. "I like that one."

"Well, I don't," Finley said stubbornly.

Demetra glared at the fox. "Then I guess I'll just have to use the Magic Mirror. It'll tell us which one to choose."

Before Finley could protest, Demetra raised the sparkling mirror above her head and chanted:

"Magic Mirror, so shiny bright,
Where is Elsinor, in dark or light?"

Once again the mirror became a liquid pool. And once again, Demetra saw Elsinor and the goblins seated on a large white mound, looking miserable.

"We need to take the little tunnel," Demetra announced. "It's obvious."

Finley peered over her shoulder. "But that's the same picture you saw before. You just wasted a turn with the mirror. Now you only have one left."

"It doesn't matter," she said as the image faded from view. "That was Elsinor, and he was clearly in the light. So I'm taking the lit tunnel."

With one last glance at the big tunnel, Finley said, "Because I am your palace advisor and protector, I must go with you."

"Suit yourself."

Demetra led the way into the little tunnel. It *was* lit, but the farther they traveled, the narrower it got. Pretty soon the princess was crawling on her hands and knees.

"I feel it's my duty to point out that you picked the wrong tunnel," Finley declared from behind her.

Demetra knew the fox was right, but she hated to admit it. She crawled forward in silence and bumped her head on the ceiling.

"I'll bet that hurt," Finley said. "If we'd taken *my* way, we'd still be walking and your head would be fine."

Demetra rubbed the top of her head and

grumbled, "You don't know that. Your tunnel could have been just as narrow."

Now Demetra was really having to struggle to fit through the passage. Her shoulders scraped against the walls, and she hit her head several more times against the ceiling.

"Oh no," she moaned as she turned a corner and nearly bumped into a stone wall that blocked the tunnel. "This is the end."

"What did I tell you?" Finley sang out.

Demetra's head hurt from hitting the rock, and she knew she'd picked the wrong tunnel. But she didn't need Finley to rub it in.

"Why does it make you happy that you're right and I'm wrong?" she hissed at Finley.

"Happy?" Finley repeated. "I'm not at all happy. I'm concerned."

"You call that concern?" Demetra replied. "You point out every mistake I make!"

The white fox seemed genuinely surprised. "But that's my job. I'm the palace advisor."

"An advisor gives advice," Demetra declared. "He doesn't criticize."

"But you won't take my advice," he replied. "Especially about Winterfest. All you do is argue with me."

Finley was right. During the planning for Winterfest he'd tried to give her suggestions, but she'd fought most of them. Then he'd called her a name.

"Why did you call me a pigheaded little princess?" Demetra asked.

There was a long silence. Finally, Finley said, "Because you had just called me a

snotty little furball, and my feelings were hurt."

Demetra winced. She forgot she *had* called him a snotty furball. And a few other names. Now she wished she hadn't.

The princess opened her mouth to apologize, but something stopped her. A low rumbling sound.

Rrrrrr!

"Did you hear that?" Finley asked.

Demetra nodded.

Rrrrrr!

"There it is again!" Finley whispered. "It sounds like snoring."

"Or growling," Demetra whispered back.

They both gulped. Hard.

"It's coming from behind that wall." Finley pointed at the rock in front of them. "I told

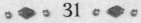

you something awful was inside this mountain."

Demetra instantly started crawling backward. "You know, Finley," she said in a very shaky voice, "you were right. We *should* have taken the big tunnel."

Finley didn't answer. He had already turned and was running full tilt for the mine entrance.

"Finley!" Demetra cried, standing up and running after him. "Where are you going?"

"Home!" Finley called over his shoulder. "I'm sorry, Princess, but I just can't stay here another minute."

At the entrance, Finley dove for the door.

But Demetra was too fast for him. She caught hold of his tail and cried, "You can't leave. We have to save Elsinor and the others."

Finley clung to the handle of the big wooden door with both paws. "Don't make me!"

"Finley, please!" Demetra tugged with all her might. "I can't do it by myself."

"Why?"

Demetra looked at the pitch-black tunnel. "Because I'm afraid of the dark!"

This took Finley by surprise, and he let go of the door. The two of them tumbled backward into the blackness of the big rock tunnel.

4

THE LONG, DARK TUNNEL

"Yeow!" Demetra hit her head on the rock wall. For a second, she saw stars. "That hurt!"

The big tunnel was pitch-black and freezing cold. Demetra felt for the wall and pulled herself to her feet.

"Finley?" she called. "Are you all right?"

No answer.

"Finley!" She reached into the darkness in front of her. "Are you there?"

Still no answer.

The goose bumps returned. They crept up her arms and down the back of her neck.

"Finley," she sang out in a quivery voice. "This isn't funny. You know I'm afraid of the dark. Now please answer me."

She held her breath and listened. Nothing.

"Maybe Finley's hurt," she whispered, "and

can't speak." She inched forward. "Don't worry, Finley. I'll find you."

The princess spread her arms out to the sides and waved them above her head. "This tunnel is enormous," she murmured. "Something very large could live in here."

The thought of something very large actually being in the tunnel with her made Demetra's heart thud faster.

"Of course," Demetra called in a high voice, "if something large *was* in here, it would let me know. Wouldn't it?"

She waited for an answer. But none came.

"Good." The princess heaved a sigh of relief. "For a moment there, I thought Finley's story about the scary thing inside the mountain might be true."

She chuckled to herself, turned, and froze.

Just ahead was a thin beam of light. It stretched from the ceiling to the tunnel floor.

"That must be some kind of window to the outside," Demetra murmured.

But the light didn't just touch the floor. It went *through* it. If Demetra had been looking down, she would have noticed that.

Instead, her head was tilted upward as she stepped into the beam of light. "Sky!" she gasped. "That looks like— *Helllllllllp!*"

Demetra tumbled head over heels through the large hole in the tunnel floor.

Glowing crystals sparkled all around the princess. They were as bright as stars on a clear night.

Demetra held her breath, waiting to crash into hard rock.

But just as she was about to hit the ground, two large hands reached out for her.

They were bright purple and covered in tiny green spots.

5

THE CRYSTAL CAVE

"Caught you!" a male voice croaked as Demetra fell into his outstretched arms. "Princess, are you all right?"

The green mist was thicker than ever, and Demetra could hardly see.

"Elsinor?" she asked, leaning her face closer to her rescuer's. "Is that you?"

The goblin leader had bright red eyes, two pointed lavender ears, and a bushy tuft

of green hair that exploded out of the top of his head.

He smiled at her, revealing two large fangs. "At your service."

"Have you seen Finley?" Demetra asked as Elsinor set her onto the soft white ground. "We were in a dark tunnel, and I lost him."

"I'm here," Finley called, limping through

the mist. "I fell through that hole, too. But I'm not sure where *here* is."

"I believe we're at the heart of Sparkle Mountain," a small, round goblin named Crag replied. "We fell into this crystal cave this morning."

"How did it happen?" Demetra asked.

"We were mining for crystal in that big, dark tunnel," Elsinor explained, "when Tor broke a hole through the rock."

Tor nodded vigorously. "The floor crumbled around our feet. I fell through the hole first. Then Crag, then Adit, and finally everyone followed me."

Elsinor stomped his foot on the soft white ground. "We landed on this strange grassy hill."

"And we've been stuck here ever since," Crag finished.

"There must be some way to get out of here," Finley said, scanning the sparkling walls of the cave. "A door or a crack in the crystal."

Elsinor shook his head. "We've looked. The only way out is the way we came in." He pointed upward. "Through that hole."

Demetra looked up. She could see the opening in the roof of the cave. Beyond that, at the end of a long, narrow shaft, she could just glimpse a bit of blue.

"Is that the sky?" she asked.

"Yes," Adit replied. "That's an air shaft. We used it to send for help."

"You mean you made that green cloud?" Finley asked.

"With this." Elsinor showed them a small glass bottle of glowing green liquid.

"He mixed peridot ore with water to

create a mist," Crag explained. "Then we fanned it through that hole."

"Your signal worked," the princess said. "We saw the green cloud and rushed to see what was the matter."

"But the fog was so thick, we could barely find the path up the mountain," Finley added.

Elsinor smiled sheepishly. "I wasn't sure how much ore to use." He coughed and batted at the mist swirling around his face. "I'm afraid I overdid it."

Finley leaned forward and whispered, "I've always heard that something very large and very frightening lives inside this mountain."

"I've heard that story, too," Elsinor whispered back. "But I've never seen anything."

"I'm very glad to hear it," Finley said, putting one paw to his heart.

Suddenly, the mound began to tremble.

"What's going on?" Demetra cried, her teeth clattering together. "It feels like an earthquake."

"Don't panic," Crag said as he steadied the princess with one purple hand. "Sometimes the ground will shake for minutes at a time."

"And sometimes it makes a deep rumbling noise," Tor added. "Like snoring."

"Finley and I heard that sound," Demetra said. "I wonder what it is?"

The Diamond Princess bent down and touched the white grass at her feet. "You know, this doesn't feel like grass. It feels more like fur."

Finley patted the ground with his paws. "You're right."

The princess crawled away from the group, patting the fur as she went.

"Careful, Princess," Elsinor called through the mist. "You might slip off the hill and cut yourself on the crystal."

"I'll protect you," Finley said, hurrying to join the princess.

Demetra crawled up a furry hill and down a narrow slope. Suddenly, her hand

touched something different. It was cold and rubbery.

"Oh," she murmured, "this feels odd. Like a very large ... nose."

Demetra stretched both hands over the edge of it and grasped something smooth and pointed. "And this feels like a very sharp ... tooth."

"A hill doesn't have a nose or teeth," Finley murmured.

"Oh, Finley!" Demetra quickly backed up the slope. "This isn't a hill. It's a ... It's a ..."

Suddenly, the white ground they were standing on rose into the air, lifting them almost to the ceiling.

"BEAR!"

6

It's a Bear!

"Who is it that wakes me from my slumber?" the big bear roared.

Demetra, Finley, and the goblins clung to the beast's fur but didn't answer.

"Tell me who you are!" the big bear bellowed. "And be quick about it. I'm very tired and very hungry."

"Hungry?" Finley gasped. "Yikes!"

Elsinor spoke first. "I am Elsinor, leader of the goblins."

The big bear threw back his head and howled, "Did Lord Bleak send you?"

"Lord Bleak?" Demetra repeated. "You know him?"

"Bleak rules this kingdom," the big bear replied.

"Oh no," Demetra corrected. "He hasn't ruled here for ages. Queen Gemma and

King Regal rule the Jewel Kingdom now. They sent him away. He's far across the Dismal Sea."

The big bear slowly turned his head so his big black eyes were level with Demetra. "Who are you?"

Demetra tilted her chin up, trying to look as royal as possible. "I am Princess Demetra, the Diamond Princess. And *I* rule the White Winterland."

The big bear's eyes narrowed. "I don't believe you."

"Just ask anybody," Finley called from behind the princess. "They'll tell you it's true."

"I see no one," the big bear said with a snarl. "I speak to no one. I sleep here in this cave, a prisoner of Lord Bleak."

"Lord Bleak must have walled him in

here years ago," Elsinor whispered to the princess.

"Poor fellow," the princess whispered back.

"I wouldn't feel sorry for him," Finley hissed. "He must have done something terrible to be taken prisoner."

"What are you whispering about?" the big bear demanded.

"N-n-nothing, Mr. Bear, sir," Finley stammered. "We were just saying how this is all an unfortunate accident. We didn't mean to fall into your cave. So if you would just help us get out of here, we promise never to return."

"No one leaves this cave alive!" The big bear roared so loudly his entire body shook.

"But why?" Demetra asked, losing her balance and falling on her knees.

"If I let one of you set foot outside this cave, you'll tell Lord Bleak that I am free. And ready to fight him again."

"But there is no Lord Bleak!" Finley cried. "He's gone!"

"You're lying!" The big bear swiped at the white fox with a giant clawed foot. "I don't like liars."

Finley tried to duck, but the blow knocked him off the bear's back. He fell to the crystal floor, pinned beneath the big bear's paw.

"The bear's got Finley!" Crag cried. "What should we do?"

"Whatever it is, we'd better be quick about it," Elsinor warned. "He's crushing Finley."

Demetra didn't even pause to think. She leaped off the big bear's back and landed with a loud *thump* on the cave floor.

"Release him!" she commanded. "I can

prove that Lord Bleak no longer rules this land."

The big bear narrowed his eyes. "You can? How?"

"With my Magic Mirror." Demetra pulled the mirror from inside her jacket.

"Careful, Princess," Finley choked from under the big bear's paw. "You've already used the mirror twice. This is your last time."

"I know that," Demetra whispered back.

The princess held the sparkling mirror in front of the big bear's nose. "Well?"

The bear stared at the mirror for a long time. "All right," he said finally. "Prove it."

"I will," Demetra said. "On one condition."

The bear squinted one eye closed. "What?"

"That you let us go."

The big bear considered this for a

moment. "I'll let this fox and those goblins go," he replied. "But you, Princess, must stay."

Princess Demetra looked quickly at Finley, who was gasping for air under the bear's paw.

If she agreed, she might never see her friends and family again. But if she didn't, the bear would destroy Finley.

"All right," Demetra said with a gulp. "I'll stay."

7

THE MAGIC MIRROR

The big bear lifted Elsinor and the goblins through the hole in the cave ceiling. Then he turned to Finley.

"You're next," the big bear growled, reaching for the small white fox.

But Finley shook his head.

"If Princess Demetra stays, then I stay," he said boldly.

"Finley," Demetra said between clenched

teeth. "This is no time to be stubborn. Leave this cave and run for help."

"Elsinor can do that," Finley whispered back. "My place is with you, my friend. Whatever happens to you, happens to me."

Demetra's eyes filled with tears. "Oh, Finley, that's really very sweet."

Finley shrugged. "It's the least I can do for calling you a pigheaded princess."

"But I *was* pigheaded," Demetra confessed.

Finley twisted his fluffy white tail in his paws. "Well ... maybe just a little."

"Ahem!" The big bear cleared his throat. "Aren't you two forgetting something?"

"Sorry?" Demetra blinked her large brown eyes.

"The Magic Mirror," the big bear growled impatiently. "You were going to show me Lord Bleak."

"No," the princess corrected. "I was going to show you King Regal and Queen Gemma. They're the rulers of the Jewel Kingdom."

The bear slammed one huge paw onto the ground, spraying bits of broken crystal everywhere. "I want to see Lord Bleak!"

Demetra had never seen Lord Bleak, but she had heard that he was awful to look at.

"I don't know if I can stand to look at him," she replied in a tiny voice. "Maybe *you* should use the mirror."

She offered the glittering mirror to the big bear.

He reached for it, then quickly withdrew his paw. "What is this," he snarled, "some kind of trick? I'm not touching that mirror."

"You can touch it," Demetra assured the big bear. "It won't hurt you."

To prove it, Finley reached for the shimmering glass. "See? It's easy." He raised the mirror in the air and explained, "You simply say, *Magic Mirror, so shiny bright*, then wish for something you'd like to see."

"That's right." Demetra nodded.

With the mirror still in the air, Finley

said, "I'll tell you what I'd like to see. I'd like to see the Winterfest Parade. With all our friends from the White Wonderland. If I could just have one last glimpse of them, I'd be happy."

Suddenly, the diamonds on the handle began to sparkle, and the mirrored glass turned into a silver reflecting pool.

"Finley!" Demetra gasped. "What have you done? That was the third wish. There are no more."

Finley slowly turned to face the big bear. He held out the Magic Mirror and murmured, "Oops."

8

JOIN THE PARADE!

The big bear was about to smash the Magic Mirror against a rock when something he saw stopped him.

"That looks like my old friend Charger," he murmured. "But that's not possible."

Princess Demetra peered over his paw at the image in the mirror. A white winged horse was leading a parade of people carrying torches and silver banners.

"That *is* Charger," Demetra cried. "He's

leading the Winterfest Parade. Oh, look!" she gasped, pointing to the three princesses behind the winged horse. "Those are my cousins Roxanne, Emily, and Sabrina."

The big bear turned to her in amazement. "Charger is my oldest and dearest friend. Together we tried to stop Lord Bleak. But we couldn't do it." The big bear looked back at the image. "We were separated when Bleak took us prisoner. I thought Charger was dead."

"Charger escaped," Finley explained. "He fought twenty of Bleak's terrible Dreadlings to do it." The fox pointed at the horse in the mirror. "You can see his battle scars there, across his chest."

"So what you say is true," the big bear cried. "Lord Bleak is banished."

Demetra nodded vigorously. "He's far across the Dismal Sea."

"And the evil Dreadlings?"

"They were packed off with him," Finley added. "Now everyone in our kingdom is free and happy."

"Then I can come out," the big bear said softly.

"And see your friends," Demetra added. "You're free now."

Two huge teardrops formed in the big bear's eyes. Finley and Demetra managed to leap out of the way as the tears dripped off the tip of his nose and splashed onto the cave floor.

"Oh dear," Demetra exclaimed. "I hope those aren't tears of sadness."

"No, no," the big bear said, shaking his head. "They are tears of joy. How I've dreamed of this day! But I never thought it could happen."

Finley, who was busy watching the action in the mirror, suddenly said, "I thought the Winterfest Parade was supposed to circle the lake and return to the castle."

"It is," Demetra replied.

"They've left the lake," Finley observed. "And now they're marching up here. Toward Sparkle Mountain."

"Look at their faces," Demetra said. "They don't look happy. They look worried."

"Look at Charger," the big bear added. "He's no longer marching, he's flying. And one of those purple goblins is on his back."

"They're coming to rescue us!" Demetra cried. She looked at Finley and whispered, "We made a promise to stay here with the big bear. We've got to stop them."

 67

"Why stop them?" the big bear declared, rearing up on his hind legs. With his huge paw he punched a bigger hole in the cave's roof. "Let's join them."

"You mean we're free to go?" Finley asked.

The big bear chuckled. "Of course. We're all free!"

Then he reached behind a crystal boulder and pulled out a big red collar. It was studded with sparkling diamonds.

"Help me put this on, will you?" he asked, dropping it in front of Demetra. "I want to look my best when I greet Charger."

Demetra read the name on the collar. "Bernard. Is that your name?"

"Why, yes, it is," the big bear replied, with a bow of his head. "Bernard Bear. And I am very pleased to make your acquaintance, Princess Demetra. And yours, too, Mr. Finley."

While Bernard Bear told his tale of being imprisoned in the crystal cave and sleeping for years, Finley and Demetra worked to make him look presentable.

They buckled the collar around his neck. Then Demetra untangled the knots in his fur, and Finley smoothed the hair around his face.

When they'd finished, Demetra clapped

her hands together. "Oh, Bernard, you look magnificent!"

"Why, thank you," Bernard replied. "Now if you two will climb onto my back, we'll join the parade."

"Will we have to go back through that dark tunnel?" Demetra asked, glancing skyward.

Bernard nodded his huge head. "It's the only way out."

Demetra gulped.

"Don't worry, Princess," Finley whispered in her ear, "I'll hold your hand."

Demetra smiled at the fox and murmured, "Thanks, friend."

Minutes later, Bernard Bear appeared at the mine entrance. Princess Demetra and Finley were waving merrily from his back.

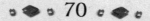

The cheer that rose up from the waiting crowd was deafening.

A shrill whinny split the air as Charger recognized his old friend and flew to meet Bernard.

Once Demetra and Finley were safely on the ground, Princess Sabrina rushed forward. She was followed by Emily and Roxanne.

"Are you all right?" Sabrina cried breathlessly.

"We were so worried," Emily said, hugging Demetra.

"When Elsinor told us that a giant bear was holding you prisoner," Roxanne cut in, "we came as fast as we could."

"We were afraid the bear might have eaten you," Sabrina said with a frown.

"Oh no." Demetra chuckled. "He would never do that. He doesn't like meat."

"Bernard told us he only eats fruits and nuts," Finley added. "And I must say I was very glad to hear that."

Sabrina looked from Demetra to Finley. And back again. Finally, she asked, "You and Finley? Are you ...?"

"Are we what, Sabrina?" Demetra asked with a twinkle in her eye.

"Are you still ... you know." Sabrina shrugged with frustration. "Fighting?"

Demetra and Finley looked at each other and started giggling.

"I believe I can answer your question," Finley said, taking Demetra by the hand. "Though the Diamond Princess can some-times be a little pigheaded—"

"And though Finley has occasionally behaved like a snotty little furball," Demetra added. "We are now—"

"And will always be," Finley cut in.

They smiled at each other and declared, "Best friends forever!"

Read the first sparkling adventure in
the Jewel Kingdom series!

JEWEL KINGDOM

The Ruby Princess
Runs Away

Turn the page for a special sneak peek!

1

ROXANNE RUNS AWAY

"I can't do it," Roxanne whispered from her hiding place in the royalberry tree. "I can't be a Jewel Princess. I'm not ready."

Today was the day she and her cousins would be crowned in a coronation ceremony.

It was also the day they would leave the Jewel Palace, where they had grown up.

As the Ruby Princess, Roxanne would have to move to her new castle in the Red

Mountains. The mountains lay in the far corner of the Jewel Kingdom.

"I always knew this day would come," she murmured. "I just didn't think it would come so soon."

Roxanne stared glumly down at the palace courtyard. Creatures from every land were gathering there.

Nymphs with blue skin and green hair chatted with goat-footed fauns. Richly dressed lords and ladies bowed to pointy-eared elves who rode on the shoulders of smiling giants.

"There you are!" A little red bird with a rainbow plume on his head fluttered onto the limb next to Roxanne. It was Pip, the royal secretary.

"The king and queen have been looking for you everywhere!" Pip squawked.

Queen Gemma and King Regal ruled the Jewel Kingdom. Today they were giving four of the kingdom's lands to the princesses.

"Don't tell the king and queen where I am, Pip," Roxanne pleaded. "I can't face them. Not yet."

"The ceremony is about to begin." Pip tapped Roxanne's hand with his long yellow beak. "Everybody from the Jewel Kingdom is here."

Roxanne's big brown eyes widened. "Everybody?"

"Everybody who's anybody." Pip ticked off the names of the guests on one wing. "There are the gnomes, the craghoppers, and the pixies from the Red Mountains."

Roxanne gulped.

"Then there are all those creatures from the Greenwood, Blue Lake, and the White Winterland."

Those were her cousins' lands.

"Then there are the young knights of Bronze, Silver, Iron, and—"

"Stop!" Roxanne pinched Pip's beak closed. "If you're trying to make me nervous," she whispered, "you are doing a very good job."

Pip shook his beak free from her grasp. He hopped to the limb above Roxanne's head.

"You shouldn't be nervous," Pip said. "You should be excited, like your cousins."

Roxanne's cousin Emily had been up since dawn, chattering about being crowned the Emerald Princess.

Demetra, the Diamond Princess, had spent the entire week in front of her mirror nervously brushing and brushing her shiny black hair.

Sabrina, the Sapphire Princess, was usually the quietest of the four. But even she had rattled on about sprites and striders and all the new friends she would make at Blue Lake.

Every princess but Roxanne was happy.

"I just don't feel like a princess," she said with a huge sigh. "In fact, I feel very ordinary."

"Careful!" Pip glanced nervously at the palace windows. "Someone might hear you."

But, Pip, look at me." Roxanne stood up in the crook of the tree. "I'm just a regular girl. I like to climb trees, ride horses, and go swimming."

"That will change," Pip murmured.

"I don't like dresses." Roxanne gestured to her beautiful red-velvet gown. "I'd rather wear pants."

Pip winced. "Heaven forbid."

"And how can I rule and protect the people of the Red Mountains when I can't protect myself?"

Roxanne showed Pip her leg. Her stockings were torn. And a very large lump had formed on her shin. "I banged my knee on the palace wall when I climbed up here."

Pip fluttered in circles around the tree. "Oh dear, oh dear!"

Roxanne tilted her head. "How does a person rule, anyway?"

"How should I know?" Pip ruffled his feathers. "You just order people around."

"Order people around." Roxanne wrinkled her nose. "That doesn't sound like fun."

"Who said being a princess was fun?" Pip squawked.

Ta-ra ta-ra ta-ra!

The trumpets sounded at the front gate. The palace guard announced, "Presenting the great wizard Gallivant!"

"Gallivant!" Roxanne gasped, nearly falling out of the tree.

The wizard was very old and very powerful. Just hearing his name made Roxanne weak in the knees.

"There he is." Below her, Roxanne could see the big white plumes of the horses that pulled the wizard's gleaming glass coach.

Pip flew to a ledge in the courtyard to get a closer look. He called to the princess, "Gallivant is carrying the Great Jeweled Crown!"

The crown held the royal jewels of the kingdom. Four jewels from this crown would be given to the princesses today.

Roxanne watched everyone in the court-yard bow low as the wizard passed.

"Soon they'll be bowing to me," Roxanne murmured. "I'll be in a coach with the Ruby Crown on my head. The coach will take me far away from my family and friends. And there I'll sit all by myself in some lonely old castle..."

Roxanne's voice trailed off. The palace gates were standing wide open.

Her eyes widened. *I don't have to be crowned today*, she thought. *I could just leap out of this tree and run away.*

Pip flew back to her. "Hurry, my lady. You must join the king and queen and your cousins. They're about to greet the wizard."

Ta-ra ta-ra ta-ra!

The trumpets sounded again.

"It's now or never," Roxanne said, keeping her eyes fixed on the open gate.

Queen Gemma and King Regal stepped onto the marble steps of the palace. A cheer rang from every creature in the courtyard.

Roxanne gathered her skirts around her, took a deep breath, and leaped. "Now!"

Who says princesses have to be perfect?

Puppy Princess — Party Time!
Patty Furlington
SCHOLASTIC

Puppy Princess — Super Sweet Dreams
Patty Furlington
SCHOLASTIC

Puppy Princess — Wish Upon a Star
Patty Furlington
SCHOLASTIC

Puppy Princess — Flower Girl Power
PATTY FURLINGTON
SCHOLASTIC

Join Princess Rosie and Cleo the Kitten as they go on fun adventures around Petrovia!

SCHOLASTIC
scholastic.com